Suzie Saves the Day

the Day

(Based on a True Story)

Suzie

Stacy Kreycik Miller

Creative Designers:
Madisen Randa and Chase Orsborn

ISBN 978-1-64003-594-2 (Paperback)
ISBN 978-1-64003-595-9 (Digital)

Covenant Books, Inc.
11661 Hwy 707
Murrells Inlet, SC 29576
www.covenantbooks.com

I lovingly dedicate this book to my father, Kenard Frank Kreycik, who developed and operated Kreycik Elk & Buffalo Ranch along the scenic Niobrara River Valley near Niobrara, Nebraska. He followed his dream and his passion to develop a unique ranch where he raised cattle, elk, and buffalo. My father was a caring and giving man who would be there to help anyone with anything they needed. I'm so grateful for the love and passion he had for his family and animals and that he passed those qualities on to my brother and me. It was from him we learned about working hard to fulfill our dreams and to remember that giving and helping others is always more rewarding than receiving.

My father Kenard F. Kreycik passed away in 2012. The Kreycik Elk & Buffalo Ranch has continued as a family working ranch, where educational covered-wagon tours are still being given. My father's memory lives on through the family-ranch operations, through the tours, and, of course, his pet cow elk Suzie who still lives on the ranch.

uzie is a sweet, kind, and obedient little elk. She always does the right thing to stay safe and to honor her owner, Farmer Frank.

Farmer Frank raised Suzie from a bottle calf because the elk mother could not give her the milk she needed. Farmer Frank brought Suzie into his house to care for her and feed her every four hours until she was big enough to go live with the rest of the herd. While he held Suzie and fed her special milk from a bottle, he would rub her ears and talk softly to her. Soon she became tame and followed him around like a pet. They were like family. Suzie knew Farmer Frank would always take care of her and the rest of the elk.

Farmer Frank fed all the elk every day and loved them all so much. He built a fence to keep them safe from predators or hunters that could hurt Suzie and her elk family.

The elk's home was a lush green pasture with beautiful trees and a creek with fresh water running through it. Suzie knew Farmer Frank built a fence around the pasture to keep them safe inside. However, there was another elk in the herd named Sally. She was a mischievous little elk and very curious. She always wondered what was on the other side of the fence.

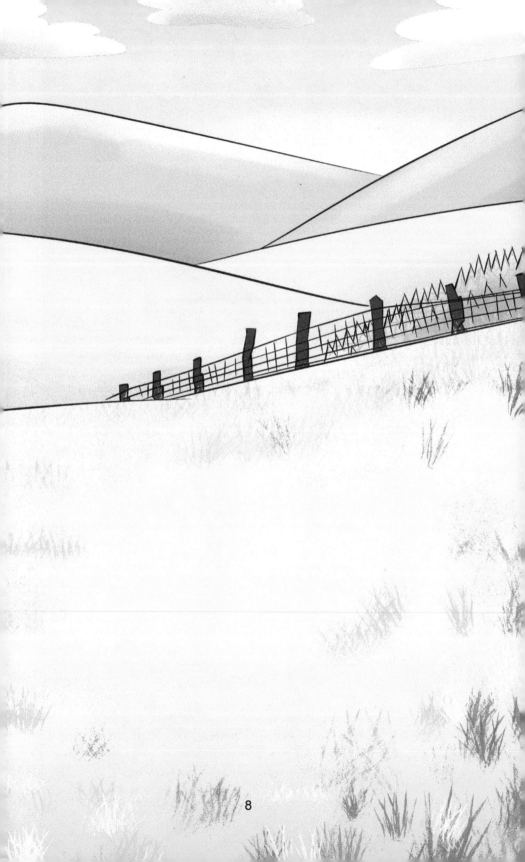

Finally, one day, Sally found a way to open the *gate*! She called to all the other elk to follow her to the outside where there were miles of wide open spaces to run and explore. The herd began to move toward the gate.

Suzie was worried! She yelled, "Wait everyone, don't go! You don't know what's out there! There could be hunters or predators ready to hurt us! How do we even know if there is food out there? We might get lost. Please don't go!"

Sally shouted to the herd, "Who cares, let's just go! Come *on*!"

13

Suzie was scared, but she followed anyway. She hoped she could help keep the herd together because she knew Farmer Frank would surely come to look for them. If they stayed together, he could bring them all home together.

The herd ran for a long way until they finally stopped. They had no idea where they were or how far they had gone. Now they were lost.

That was not their only problem. A pack of coyotes began to circle the herd. Suzie warned the others about the danger. Sally reminded the herd to use their front feet as weapons and strike at the coyotes.

They struck at two snarling coyotes, and that was enough to frighten them away.

Even after the coyotes ran off, Sally was still scared and told the others, "I'm so sorry, we should have listened to Suzie and stayed home where it was safe. Can you all forgive me for leading you out here into danger?"

Just then Suzie heard Farmer Frank in the distance hollering her name. "Hey, everyone, you hear that? It's Farmer Frank. He came looking for us!" shouted Suzie. Suzie led the other elk toward Farmer Frank who was calling, "Here, Suz. Come on, girl!"

It wasn't long before they met up with Farmer Frank. Both Farmer Frank and Suzie were so excited to see each other. "Suz, you scared me," said Farmer Frank. "Please don't ever run away again. Stay here where I can keep you safe." Suzie rubbed her nose on Farmer Frank's arm, letting him know she understood. The rest of the herd was also very happy to see him

Sally said, "I should have been happy to stay here where Farmer Frank feeds us and keeps us safe. I'm staying right here on the ranch from now on!"

"Me too!" agreed Suzie and the rest of the elk.

Just as Farmer Frank kept Suzie and the herd safe in their pasture with a fence, God keeps us safely tucked in his loving spiritual arms.

Kenard Kreycik (Farmer Frank) and three-year-old
grandson Jace bottle-feeding week-old elk calf Suzie.

Kreycik with his pet elk Suzie by the
covered wagon during a tour.

Elk herd bull with his harem of cows on a hilltop overlooking the Niobrara River at Kreycik Elk & Buffalo Ranch near Niobrara, Nebraska.

Kenard Frank Kreycik (Farmer Frank)
February 8, 1946 – October 24, 2012

Acknowledgments

Thank you to my mom and aunt for all the support and love and not giving up on me. Thank you, Sharon, for all your advice, editing, and encouragement in making my dream possible.

About the Author

Stacy Kreycik Miller was fortunate to have been raised in a family that incorporated farming and ranching, which included cattle as well as elk and bison, near Niobrara, Nebraska. There, her father, Kenard Frank Kreycik, and mother, Chris, instilled in her the value of hard work, respect, and love for the land, including all the creatures that inhabit it. Stacy continued to work on learning more about ranching/farming by attending Wayne State College and earned a BS in agriculture business.

Helping to build, grow, and run her family's tour business is only one of Stacy's passions. She has been married to her best friend Clint for seventeen years and is a mother to their three awesome children, Jace, Josilyn and Jaeli. Stacy leads a busy family life that includes supporting her children's school events. She also regularly helps Clint with their own cow/calf herd. Stacy is blessed to have Jesus Christ as her Lord and Savior. She is active in her church and teaches Sunday school.

Another of Stacy's passions is writing stories. *Suzi Saves the Day* is her first published book. She hopes to share both her and her father's love and passion for animals and the land with the readers.

You can contact Stacy at: www.nebraskaelktours.com

CPSIA information can be obtained
at www.ICGtesting.com
Printed in the USA
BVHW06s0038190918
527790BV00001B/1/P